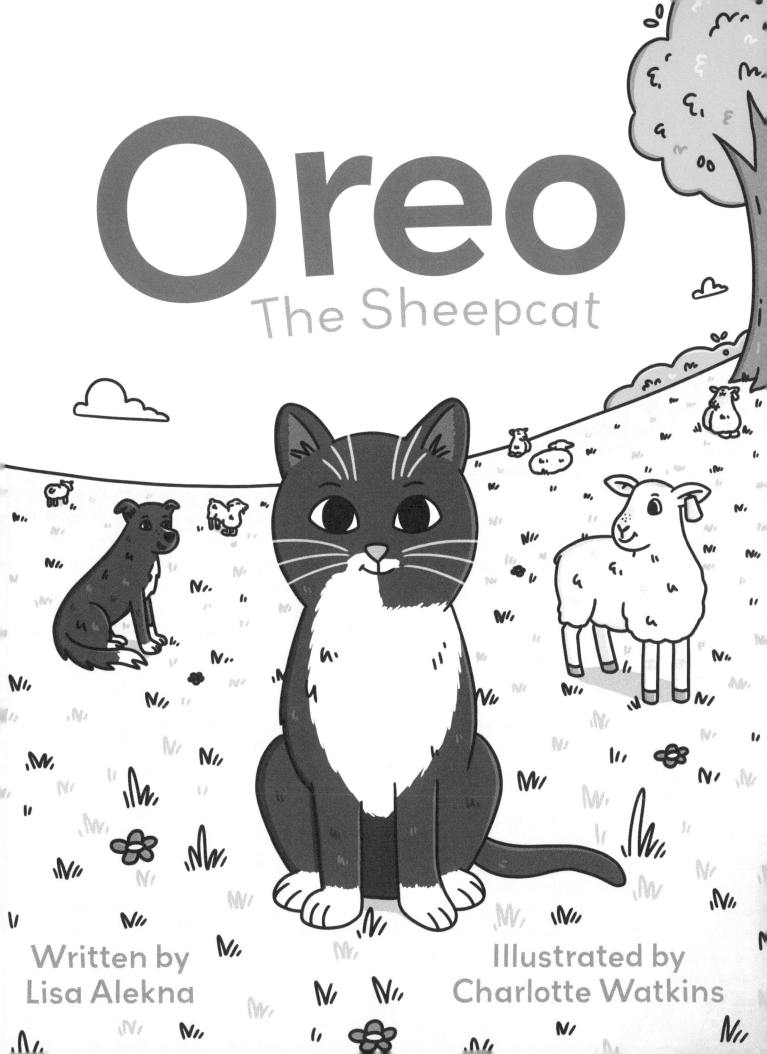

Oreo
The Sheepcat

Written by
Lisa Alekna

Illustrated by
Charlotte Watkins

In memory of Marshall,
who made all this happen
and taught us so much.

Published in the United Kingdom by:

Blue Falcon Publishing
The Mill, Pury Hill Business Park,
Alderton Road, Towcester
Northamptonshire NN12 7LS
Email: books@bluefalconpublishing.co.uk
Web: www.bluefalconpublishing.co.uk

A CIP record of this book is available from the British Library.

First printed June 2022
ISBN 9781912765607

Oreo the

Sheepcat

Lisa Alekna

Meet Twig's friend Oreo, a tuxedo cat.
A cat that had trouble with being... a CAT!

He'd sleep on the toilet, instead of a lap,
And get up to mischief, instead of a nap.

He'd follow the vacuum, splash round a hose,

Play with the dogs... With no fear of all those

The other cats teased him and kept well away.
They wouldn't let Oreo join them or play.

He just didn't fit
the cat stereotype.
One paw too near them,
he's met with a swipe.

But Twig's sheepdog Marshall saw Oreo sad.
Decided he needed to help the poor lad.
To cheer him up, Marshall taught him to dance,
Performing a rather peculiar prance!

Then Marshall took Oreo under his wing.

From that day on began sheepdog training.

Day one of training: STOP BEING A CAT.

(We all know he didn't have trouble with that.)

Day two of training: BEING A DOG,
Which seemed to come easy for this failed mog.

He was taught how to sit and the perfect recall,

How to play tug, and how to play ball,

How to run like a dog,

how to bound,

how to stalk,

And how to enjoy a
long morning dog walk.

BECOMING A DOG mastered: eat, play and sleep.
So now it was time to introduce sheep!
This is where Marshall found training quite tough.
He'd just get distracted by all kinds of stuff.

He'd get too excited, or look the wrong way,
and sometimes he'd sneak off to sleep in the hay!
Perhaps being a sheepdog was not meant to be,
So Oreo tried out new things just to see.

We've mentioned the dancing: he's not good enough,
So then he tried modelling for cat food and stuff.

But Mum's photo shoots quickly proved Oreo's
Modelling would be for how not to pose.

So he then tried gymnastics, but it was too dangerous.
Turns on barbed wire were just ludicrous.

He then helped to homeschool, and learned of painting,
And that's how PICATSSO became the next thing.
Until he got paw prints all over the room
And was chased out of the house by his mum with a broom.

The next day he shocked the lovely postman
By being the black and white cat in his van!
Then the plumber, the builder, the Gardener Chris,
But none of them needed a cat apprentice.

Oreo quickly ran out of ideas.

He just wasn't suitable for these careers.

'Til one day when Marshall was earning his keep,
Oreo noticed him working the sheep.
He copied his teacher herding the flock,
As other cats watched him, unable to mock.

The walk up, the stand, the come bye and away,

Oreo put on a unique display.

Sheepdog and sheepcat worked as a team.

Sheepdog now mastered (or so it would seem)!

He brings new techniques to the sheep herding.
Some are quite helpful, but most... hindering.

But Marshall's shown Oreo what he wants to be:
SHEEPCAT! The best one you ever will see.

GAMES

Can you help Oreo get the sheep to their matching coloured pens?

Can you find Oreo on the farm?

Can you find Marshall on the farm?

Can you find Twig on the farm?

What else can you find?

Test Your Knowledge

1. What animal is Oreo?

2. What animal did Oreo want to be?

3. What animal is Oreo's friend Twig?

4. Do cats have fur or wool?

5. Oreo is a black cat with white chest and socks.

What name is given to a cat that looks like Oreo?

6. What 3 things are cats normally scared of, but Oreo isn't?

7. Do you think Oreo has lots of fun with Marshall and Twig?

8. Do you think Marshall is a good brother to Oreo?

9. What is your favourite animal?

10. What would you like to be?

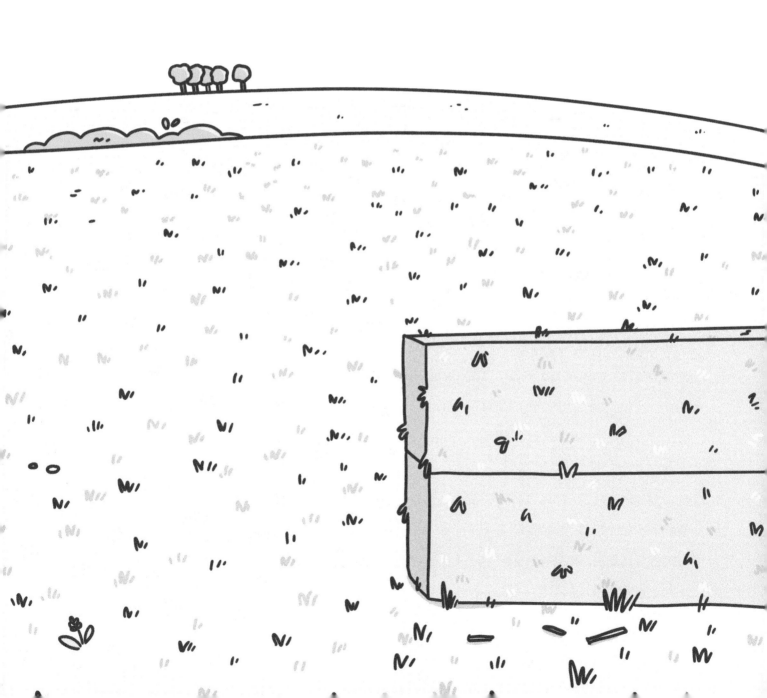

About the Author

As a mother of two boys, Lisa has always treasured the bedtime story, particularly rhyming catchy picture books, where her boys marvel at the illustrations, get engrossed in the characters, and enjoy the rhythm of the poetry.

Lisa has always enjoyed writing poems and hoped to create a children's book for others to enjoy one day. So when her border collie pup found his way into the world of sheep and saw Lisa begin her very own hobby farm, it wasn't long before the characters of her book were born and pen was put to paper.

The release of 'Little Twig's Big Adventures' last year, tells the true story of a tiny bottle lamb that beat all odds of not only surviving his first night, but also the endless escapes to find his Shepherd and Sheepdog. The release of her second book, sees Marshall the sheepdog returning once more, but this time in the form of a career's adviser, teacher and guardian... to a cat.

The true story of how Lisa's sheepdog that started it all, took Oreo, a cat that struggles with being a cat, under his wing to help find what makes him happy!

The unlikely duo, and charismatic cat Oreo, have provided their family with many smiles, gasps and laughs, which Lisa has now captured in a book for you all to enjoy.

I wonder who will be in the next story?

Other Books by the Author

Little Twig's Big Adventures

Little Twig longs to be bigger and faster, just like all the other lambs in his field.

Lonely and sad, he sets off in search of his only friends, the shepherd and her sheepdog, to find a place he can finally fit in. But when the rest of the flock learn of Twig's adventures, they begin to see the little lamb in a way they never have before!

Join Twig and his friends in this heart-warming rhyming story.

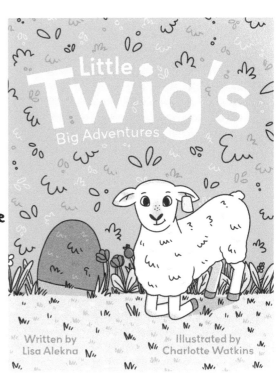

Lightning Source UK Ltd.
Milton Keynes UK
UKHW050634290622
405112UK00005B/53